The Boxcar Children® Mysteries

THE CEREAL BOX MYSTERY

created by
GERTRUDE CHANDLER WARNER

Illustrated by Charles Tang

ALBERT WHITMAN & Company
Morton Grove, Illinois

Library of Congress Cataloging-in-Publication Data
is available from the Library of Congress.

ISBN 0-8075-1114-5 (hardcover)
ISBN 0-8075-1115-3 (paperback)

Cover art by David Cunningham.

Contents

CHAPTER 1

A Box of Silver Frosted Stars

Mrs. McGregor was making a list for the Alden children to take to the grocery store. "Anything else?" she asked.

"Cereal!" cried Benny Alden. "You didn't forget the Silver Frosted Stars, did you?"

Mrs. McGregor looked at the grocery list. "No, I didn't, Benny. Your favorite cereal is right at the top of the list."

She handed the list to fourteen-year-old Henry Alden. He folded it and put it in his pocket.

"I just need two more silver stars from inside the cereal boxes," Benny said. "Then I can send away for my very own silver star detective's badge."

Twelve-year-old Jessie Alden laughed. "We know, Benny," she said.

Violet, who was ten, smiled at her six-year-old brother. "Even if you don't find a star inside the cereal, you'll find a prize, won't you, Benny?" she asked.

Benny nodded. Then he said, "If it is a really good prize, maybe I will give it to Grandfather for his birthday."

The others laughed. Their dog, Watch, who was curled up on his dog bed near the door, stood up. He wagged his tail and barked.

"No, Watch, you can't come with us," Henry said. "We're riding our bikes and it is too hot for you to run alongside."

"But we'll bring you a present," Benny promised. He petted the dog on the head.

"Yes. A brand-new col —" Jessie began, but Benny stopped her.

Benny put his hands over Watch's ears. "Shhh! It's supposed to be a surprise! You have to keep your lips zipped!" Benny pretended he was zipping his lips shut.

"Right," said Jessie, and pretended to zip her own lips shut, too.

Saying good-bye to Mrs. McGregor and Watch, the Aldens got on their bicycles and rode through the streets of Greenfield to the grocery store downtown.

In the cereal aisle of the grocery store, Benny went straight to the Silver Frosted Stars. He studied all the boxes closely. He took each box off the shelf and gave it a gentle shake. Finally, he said, "This is a good box." He put the cereal in the shopping cart.

Henry pushed the cart a little way down the grocery aisle.

"Wait!" said Benny. He held up two more boxes. "These are good boxes, too."

He looked hopefully at his brother and two sisters. "We could get three boxes of Silver Frosted Stars," he said. "I promise to eat all three."

"Oh, Benny! Three boxes?" said Jessie.

But Violet, who always liked to be help-

ful, said, "I could help you eat the cereal, too, Benny."

Henry and Jessie exchanged glances. Henry said, "I guess I could eat a few bowls of Silver Frosted Stars."

"Me, too," Jessie agreed.

"Hooray!" cried Benny, and he skipped happily to the shopping cart to add two more boxes of his favorite cereal.

The moment they had left the grocery store, Benny opened one of the boxes of cereal. "Look!" he cried. "A silver star! Now I only need one more to send away for my special detective's badge."

"Good for you, Benny," Henry said as he and Jessie loaded grocery bags into the baskets of the bicycles. "But you can't open any more boxes of cereal until you finish that one."

"I'll start right now," Benny said. He took a handful of cereal from the box and began to eat it.

"No milk, Benny?" asked Violet.

Benny grinned. "It tastes good this way, too!" he assured her.

They walked along Main Street, past the hardware store and the bookstore. Outside the bakery, Benny stopped and pointed. "Look at that cake," he said.

"It's a beautiful cake," said Jessie.

Benny put the box of cereal back in the bag in one of the bicycle baskets.

"It's a birthday cake," said Henry. "A cake like that would be nice for Grandfather's birthday."

Violet said, "Mrs. McGregor could make a cake like that, especially if we helped."

"With a cake like that, you need a party," said Jessie.

The four Aldens looked at one another. Then Henry said, "Is anyone else thinking what I'm thinking?"

"A party!" Benny crowed. "We can have a party for Grandfather's birthday."

"A surprise party," Jessie said. "Let's make it a big surprise."

Violet said, "We can invite Soo Lee and Cousin Alice and Cousin Joe."

Everyone began to talk at once. They

were so excited that they almost forgot about Watch's surprise.

Then Jessie said, "Oh, dear. We just passed the pet supply store!"

They turned their bikes around and walked them back to the pet store. They parked their bikes outside and went in.

Benny and Violet chose a new red collar for Watch and even ordered him a new tag with his name and address and phone number on it. As they walked out of the store, Benny said, "It's too bad the tags aren't shaped like stars. Then Watch could be a detective, too."

Ahead of Benny, Jessie stopped so suddenly that Benny bumped into her.

"Ow!" said Benny.

"Look out!" Henry said.

"Police! Stop! Stop, thief!" they heard a voice cry.

CHAPTER 2

The Stolen Rubies

A police officer raced past the Aldens, almost crashing into Henry. She didn't even see him.

The police officer disappeared around the corner.

The Aldens looked back in the direction from which the officer had come. They saw a man and a woman standing outside an antiques store. The woman pointed and the man waved his arms in excitement.

"There must have been a robbery," Jessie said. "Let's go find out."

The Aldens hurried up to the two people outside the store. "What happened?" Jessie asked as they got closer.

The woman turned. She was a short woman, not much taller than Henry, with round blue eyes and long dark brown hair pulled into a French braid. Strands of hair were sticking out from the braid and one sleeve of her shirt was torn. "A robbery!" she gasped. "I tried to stop him, but he got away. He tore my shirt!"

"Did the robber wear a mask?" asked Benny.

The man shook his head. He was a small, thin man wearing thick glasses. "I'm Will Bellows. I own Antique Treasures." He pointed to the sign above the shop. "This thief was quite bold. He just grabbed something and ran out when I was helping Ms. Smitts here and another customer. Ms. Smitts was very brave. She ran after the thief and caught him right outside the door, but he pulled free."

"What did he look like?" asked Henry.

Ms. Smitts said, "I don't know . . . it all

happened so fast. He wasn't very tall. But he had a hat pulled low over his forehead and a scarf pulled up around the lower part of his face. He might have had a mustache. He pushed me away and ran."

Mr. Bellows couldn't remember, either. "He stayed in the darkest part of the shop," he said. "And he kept his shoulders hunched and his face turned away. He had on a tan raincoat and a brown hat, but that's all I remember. I only noticed the raincoat because it wasn't raining outside. I thought that it was odd."

"What was stolen?" Violet asked.

Mr. Bellows clapped his hand to his forehead. "The rings!" he said. "I left the tray of rings I was showing to a customer right out on the counter."

Turning, Mr. Bellows rushed back into his shop with the Aldens and Ms. Smitts behind him. Inside, they found a small room filled with all kinds of old furniture, lamps, and books. A glass case displayed jewelry. An anxious-looking young man with round wire-rimmed glasses was hovering near one end of the glass case.

"Did you catch the thief?" the man asked.

"Not yet," Mr. Bellows said.

"Who are you?" Benny asked.

The man peered at Benny through his glasses and said, "I'm David. David Darden. I'm trying to find an engagement ring." He blushed slightly. Then he said to Benny, "Who are you?"

"I'm Benny Alden," Benny said.

Meanwhile, Mr. Bellows had hurried over to the blue velvet tray at David's elbow. "They're all here," he said, sounding relieved. "All the rings are still here!"

Now David Darden looked surprised and a little hurt. "Of course they are. I stayed in the shop to make sure nothing would happen to them."

"Oh," Mr. Bellows said. He looked slightly embarrassed. "Sorry. Thank you." Then he glanced toward another corner of the store and his face grew grim. "Oh, no," he said.

"What's wrong?" asked Jessie.

"The thief took the most valuable thing in the store — a necklace set — a matching necklace, bracelet, and ring." Mr. Bellows pointed toward a small case. "They were especially valuable because they were made of rubies."

The Aldens went over to the small case. "The lock isn't broken," said Henry. "Did it have a key in it?"

"No," said Mr. Bellows. "I keep the key on my key ring."

"Could the thief have picked the lock while you were helping other customers?" asked Henry.

"It's possible," said Mr. Bellows.

"Or maybe you left it open the last time you unlocked it," Violet said.

"Oh, no. You locked it," said Mr. Darden.

"Are you sure?" asked Mr. Bellows.

"Yes," said Mr. Darden. "Right after you showed the jewels to me." He smiled and shook his head. "They were beautiful, but much too expensive for me. I just want an engagement ring."

"It's true," Ms. Smitts chimed in. "I was here when you showed the jewelry to Mr. Darden. I saw you lock the case, too."

"It's amazing that anybody could pick that lock in that short a time," said Mr. Bellows. He looked very unhappy. "They were particularly fine rubies. I was delighted when their owner offered to sell them to me."

"Rubies," Violet said softly.

"Yes," said Mr. Bellows. "And these were particularly beautiful and rare, a perfectly matched set." He sat down heavily in a nearby chair. A puff of dust came up around him, but he didn't seem to notice. "Oh, dear. Oh, dear," he said. "I hope they catch the thief."

"Don't worry," said Benny. "If they don't, we will."

Ms. Smitts laughed. Benny put his hands on his hips. "We can," he said. "We've solved lots of mysteries."

Although she stopped laughing, Ms. Smitts still kept smiling. The Aldens could tell that she didn't believe Benny.

Mr. Bellows shook his head. "If someone doesn't catch the thief," he said, "I'm ruined."

"We'd better go," said Henry. "Let us know if we can do anything to help."

Fumbling in his pocket, Mr. Bellows brought out a small notebook and a pencil. He said to Ms. Smitts and Mr. Darden, "You'd better leave your names in case the police want to talk to you."

Mr. Darden said, "Are you sure that is necessary? . . . I mean, I don't want my name to be in the newspaper."

Ms. Smitts gave Mr. Darden a suspicious look. "Well, *I* don't have anything to hide," she said. She took the notebook and pencil and wrote "Tori Smitts" and her phone number in the notebook. Reluctantly, Mr. Darden wrote in his name, address, and phone number as well.

Then Ms. Smitts and Mr. Darden walked out of the store with the Aldens. When they got outside, Benny raised his hand and pointed. "Oh, no!" he cried. "My bike. Look what happened to my bike!"

Benny's bike was no longer parked where he had left it. It was lying in the middle of the sidewalk, with groceries spilled out all around it.

Quickly the Aldens hurried toward the

bicycles. Mr. Darden and Ms. Smitts went with them. They helped the Aldens pick up the scattered cans and boxes from the grocery bag.

"There," said Ms. Smitts. She looked inside the basket and shifted the open box of Silver Frosted Stars. "It looks like one of your boxes of cereal got broken open when your bike fell over. You want me to throw it away?"

She held up the box, but Benny shook his head. "No, I'd already opened it. It's okay."

He took the box from Ms. Smitts and put it back in the basket.

"Thank you for helping us," said Henry.

"Of course," said Mr. Darden. He shook his head and smiled a little. "I guess I wasn't meant to buy an engagement ring today."

"We're just lucky no one got hurt," Ms. Smitts said. She waved at the Aldens and walked briskly away.

"Maybe I'll do a little more shopping," Mr. Darden said. He smiled again and made

his way slowly down the sidewalk, stopping to peer into the different windows.

"Wow," said Benny. "A robbery. With rubies! We've found another mystery to solve, haven't we?"

"Yes," Jessie said. "Maybe we can help Mr. Bellows."

Benny grinned. "Hooray," he said. "Now we have a party *and* a mystery!"

"Whoever took the jewels must have known they were the most valuable thing in the store," said Henry. "It had to be somebody who knew about jewelry."

"But no one even knows what he looks like," said Violet.

"The police will probably catch the thief," Henry said. But even though he said that and his brother and sisters agreed, they still talked about the mystery of the stolen rubies all the way home.

They were so busy talking that they didn't even notice the person who followed them.

CHAPTER 3

Watch Hears a Burglar

Watch pricked up his ears. He raised his head from his paws and growled softly.

"What is it, Watch?" Benny whispered, sitting up.

Watch had been sleeping at the foot of Benny's bed. It was very late. Benny could tell because the house was so quiet and dark. The only light was the night-light in Benny's bedroom.

"Grrr," growled Watch again. He hopped

off the bed and ran to Benny's bedroom door. He scratched at it.

Benny got out of bed, too. Had Watch heard something?

"Shhh," he whispered to Watch.

Watch pressed his nose against the crack beneath the door and sniffed.

Benny reached down and gripped Watch's new red collar. Slowly, quietly, he pushed the door open. Very, very carefully, he walked down the hall to Henry's room next door. He pushed Henry's door open and crept inside.

"Henry," he whispered. "Henry, wake up. I think there is a burglar in our house."

Watch growled again, more loudly. He pulled against his collar.

Henry sat up. "What?" he said sleepily. Then, realizing what Benny had said, he gasped, "A burglar?"

At that moment they heard a loud crash from downstairs. Watch barked and pulled free from Benny's grasp. Barking loudly, he ran out of the room.

"What is it?" Jessie cried. The door of

her room banged open as Henry and Benny ran past.

"Burglar," whispered Henry.

Grandfather came out into the hall and hurried after them, followed by Violet.

They heard a hoarse shout as they ran down the stairs. Then a shadowy figure ran across the hall and out the front door, with Watch at its heels. The door slammed, almost catching Watch. He yelped and jumped back, then leaped at the door again, scratching at it and barking louder than ever.

Grandfather turned on the light. A flowerpot by the front door had been turned over.

Violet and Benny ran to calm Watch.

"Good boy," Violet crooned. "You scared the burglar away."

"You're brave, Watch," said Benny, giving Watch a big hug.

Watch wagged his tail, but he gave one more soft growl, as if warning the burglar not to come back.

Henry crouched by the overturned flowerpot. "Look," he said. "The burglar left a footprint. A big footprint."

"So did Watch," Jessie added.

They studied the footprints. But although Watch's footprint was very clear, the burglar's footprint was smeared as if he had slipped. "The only thing you can tell from this footprint," Henry said at last, "is that the burglar had big feet and he was in a hurry!"

They went into the kitchen and stopped in amazement. Jessie threw out her arms. "What a mess!" she said.

Someone had broken a pane of glass in the back door and reached through it to unlock the door and come inside. Most of the cabinets had been opened. A bag of flour had been thrown on the floor, where it had burst open, coating everything in soft white powder. A loaf of bread had been knocked from the counter onto the floor.

"It doesn't look as if anything is missing," said Grandfather. "I'll call the police."

Jessie said, "Why would the thief break into the kitchen? What would he look for?"

"Maybe the thief was hungry," said Benny.

Grandfather said, "Whatever the burglar was up to, it's a good thing Watch barked when he did and scared him away."

Watch wagged his tail.

"We'll get up early and clean up this mess," Jessie said. She yawned suddenly. "I'm sleepy."

"Me, too," said Benny. He yawned also. "But we should stay awake in case the burglar comes back."

"I don't think he will, Benny," Grandfather said, patting Benny's shoulder. "And besides, Watch will be on guard."

"That's true," said Benny in a sleepy voice.

Violet shuddered. "That's two robberies in one day — at Antique Treasures and now at our house."

"But we don't have any jewelry for the thief to steal," said Benny. "He must not be a very smart burglar."

After Officer Weatherspoon from the Greenfield Police came and questioned

Grandfather about the robbery, Grandfather taped a piece of cardboard over the broken pane of glass and the Aldens went back to bed.

Everyone got up early the next morning to clean up the mess in the kitchen.

They had the kitchen almost finished when Benny stopped. His mouth dropped open.

"Benny? What's wrong?" asked Grandfather.

Benny pointed to the top of the refrigerator, where Mrs. McGregor had put his two unopened boxes of Silver Frosted Stars. "My Silver Frosted Stars," he said. "They're gone!"

"Maybe they fell behind the refrigerator," Jessie suggested. "The burglar could have bumped into it and knocked them off."

Jessie was right, but only half right. She only found one box of Silver Frosted Stars behind the refrigerator. The other box of cereal wasn't anywhere in the kitchen, or in the whole house.

"That is very strange," Henry said. "Why would anyone take a box of cereal?"

"Do you think they were collecting silver stars, too?" asked Benny.

Henry shook his head. "It doesn't seem likely."

"It doesn't make sense," Violet said.

"What we have," Jessie said, "is another mystery."

Benny frowned. "That was bad, to steal my Silver Frosted Stars."

Violet put her arm around Benny's shoulders. "Don't worry, Benny," she said. "You still have one box, as well as the one you had already opened."

Jessie looked around. "Where is that other box?" she wondered.

"In the pantry," Benny said. "Mrs. McGregor put it on a low shelf in there so I could reach it. And it's a good thing, too, or the thief might have taken it, also."

"It's okay, Benny," said Violet. "We'll get you another box of Stars."

"Okay," said Benny. He sighed. "Talking about cereal has made me hungry!"

"How many bowls of Silver Frosted Stars

are you going to eat, Benny?" asked Grandfather Alden after they'd begun eating their
breakfast.

Benny poured milk over his second bowl
of cereal. "Lots," he said. "I just need one
more silver star before I can send away for
my detective's badge. I'm almost done with
this box of cereal. Then I can open a new
one."

"I see," said Grandfather Alden. "In that
case, pass the cereal, please."

A moment later, Jessie looked around the
table and burst out laughing.

"What's so funny, Jessie?" asked Henry.

"We're all eating Benny's cereal!" she
said.

Just then Grandfather said, "Well, well,
well. What's this in my cereal?" He held
up a small ring with a big green stone in
it.

"Look what I found!" Violet exclaimed at
the same moment. "A pink ring."

Benny looked surprised. "You found two
more prizes in the cereal box? Wow, I told

you this was a good box of cereal when I picked it out at the store."

Grandfather said, "I don't think this ring will fit me."

"I think Jessie should have it," said Benny generously. "And Violet, you can have the pink ring."

Both Violet and Jessie looked pleased. They thanked Benny. Jessie's ring fit on her little finger. But Violet's was much too big for her. She had to take tape and wind it around the band so that the ring would fit. "It's a pretty pink stone," she said. "But it's heavy."

Grandfather opened the newspaper. The story of the theft was on the front page. "Look at this," he told his grandchildren. "It's about the Antique Treasures robbery."

"What does it say?" Jessie asked.

Henry leaned over his grandfather's shoulder and read, " 'Mr. Marvin Map, a known jewel thief, was captured by the police near the scene. Although Map was wearing a tan raincoat similar to the one described by witnesses, the police could find no evidence linking him to the crime. The jewels are still missing.' "

Next to the article was a photograph of Marvin Map. It showed a man with a thin face and a pointed chin and cool gray eyes.

"Oh, good," said Benny. "I'm glad they didn't catch the thief."

"Benny!" exclaimed Violet. "You don't mean that."

"No," Benny said. "I just meant that now we can help solve the mystery."

"Well, if Marvin Map didn't do it, who did?" asked Jessie.

"Maybe there were two people wearing raincoats in Greenfield yesterday," Henry suggested.

Grandfather said, "It wasn't raining yesterday. It seems unlikely that there would be two people wearing raincoats."

"True," agreed Henry.

Jessie said, "Maybe the thief hid the jewels when the police weren't looking."

"That's an idea," Henry said thoughtfully. "He could have hidden them when the police weren't right behind him. Maybe if we found out where they caught Mr. Map, we could search for the jewelry there."

"Let's go look right now!" said Benny.

"We will, Benny," Jessie said. "Just as soon as we finish our cereal!"

CHAPTER 4

Party Plans and a Mystery

"We should go to the police station and ask them where they caught Mr. Map," Henry said as they cleared the dishes from the breakfast table.

"While we are in Greenfield, we could get supplies to make decorations for Grandfather's party," Violet suggested.

"Good idea, Violet," Jessie said.

"What's this about a party?" asked Mrs. McGregor, coming into the kitchen. The Aldens told her about their plans to give their grandfather a surprise birthday party.

Mrs. McGregor thought it was a wonderful idea. She told them that she could make a cake that was even prettier than the one at the bakery. "And it will be your grandfather's favorite flavor, too," she assured them. "Chocolate with butter-cream frosting."

"And pink and lavender sugar roses?" Violet asked.

"With green sugar leaves," Mrs. McGregor added, nodding.

"We have to call Alice and Joe and Soo Lee to invite them," said Jessie. Soo Lee was the Aldens' adopted cousin from Korea. Like the Aldens, she had been an orphan, until the Aldens' cousins, Alice and Joe, had adopted her.

The Alden children had not been living in Korea when they were orphans. They had been living in an old boxcar in the woods. After their parents had died, they had run away because they had heard that their grandfather was a mean man.

But it wasn't true. He had searched and searched for them and finally found them and brought them all to live with him in his big white house in Greenfield. He had even brought the old boxcar and put it in the backyard so that they could visit it whenever they wanted.

Jessie called Soo Lee and told her about the plans for Grandfather's party. "Come over this afternoon and help us make decorations and plan it," she said.

Soo Lee agreed to ride her bike over right after lunch.

"We'd better hurry," Violet said. "We have a lot to do before Soo Lee gets here."

Leaving Watch with Mrs. McGregor, the Aldens rode their bikes into Greenfield. First they went to the police station.

Sitting at the front desk was Officer Weatherspoon, the same police officer who had come to the Aldens' house when it had been broken into.

"Marvin Map?" she repeated, when Henry asked about him. The officer shook her head. "We had to let him go for lack of evidence. He's a slippery character."

"What do you mean?" Violet asked.

Officer Weatherspoon said, "We caught

him at the intersection of Fox Lane and
Windmill Road. He was breathing heavily
as if he had been running, although he
pretended he was just walking along. He
was wearing a raincoat. We're pretty sure
he was the man who grabbed the jewelry.
But no one could make a positive identifi-
cation and we didn't find any of the jewelry
on him."

"Thank you, Officer Weatherspoon,"
Jessie said.

"Why did you want to know?" asked the
policewoman.

"We're going to find the rubies," Benny
blurted out.

Officer Weatherspoon raised her eye-
brows, but she didn't laugh. Instead she
said, "Good luck."

The Aldens got on their bicycles and
pedaled as fast as they could to the intersection of Fox Lane and Windmill Road. A
small gift shop stood on one corner. A va-
cant lot was on another. Houses were on
the other two corners.

As the Aldens got off their bikes, a huge

dog behind a fence began to bark ferociously. Benny jumped back.

Henry said, "I don't think Mr. Map hid the jewelry there!"

Pointing, Violet said, "Maybe he went into the store and hid it in there."

But when they asked the owner of the gift shop, she shook her head. "I saw the guy run by across the street," she told them. "He didn't come anywhere near my store."

"Did you see him hide anything? Or throw anything away before the police caught him?" Jessie asked.

Again the store owner shook her head. "Nope. He ran partway up the street, then stopped suddenly, put his hands in his pockets, and began to whistle as if he didn't have a care in the world. It was almost as if he wanted the police to catch him."

"Thank you," Henry said.

When they went back outside, Violet sighed. "I don't think he hid the jewels near here," she said.

"No," Jessie agreed. "But maybe we should look around, just in case."

The Aldens checked the empty lot, but all they found were tin cans, old newspapers, and one flat tire. "People sure are litterbugs," Benny said as he gathered up the garbage and put it into a trash can on the corner.

Henry bent and peered into the trash can.

"What are you doing, Henry?" Jessie asked.

"Checking to make sure he didn't hide the jewels in here. It would be a good place to hide them. Who would ever think of looking for jewels in a trash can?"

But no necklace, ring, or bracelet glittered amid the cans and bottles and papers in the garbage can.

They went to one of the corner houses and knocked on the door. When an old man answered, Violet said politely, "We're looking for something we lost. Could we check around your front yard?"

"Help yourself," the man said. "I just cut the grass two days ago, so whatever you lost should show up easily — if it's there."

"Thank you," Violet said.

They carefully searched the yard, even looking under bushes and rocks. But they didn't find the stolen jewelry. And when they knocked on the front door of the other house, no one answered.

"Let's retrace Mr. Map's steps," Henry suggested. "We saw the officer turn where the thief did. We can figure out where he went."

But although the Aldens retraced Mr. Map's escape route all the way back to Main Street, they didn't find any jewels. Nor did they find a single clue.

"Maybe he's really not the thief after all," Jessie said in a discouraged voice.

"Maybe not," Henry said.

Violet said, "Let's go talk to Mr. Bellows. We could ask him how to find Ms. Smitts and Mr. Darden, too. Maybe they could re-member something that would help us."

"Good idea," said Benny.

Mr. Bellows was sitting at the counter in his store, his chin in his hands. He did not look happy.

"Hi, Mr. Bellows," Benny said.

"What? Oh, hello," said Mr. Bellows. He didn't move.

Bending over to look at the rings sparkling on the blue velvet in the glass case, Jessie asked, "Has Mr. Darden been back to buy a ring?"

"No," said Mr. Bellows. He made a face. "My last customer was the thief. And he wasn't exactly a paying customer."

"Have you remembered anything else about the robbery?" Henry asked. "Something else that might help catch the thief?"

"Not a thing," said Mr. Bellows. "I just bought those rubies recently. How could the thief have known about them?"

"Maybe he had been in your shop before. Maybe he saw them then," Violet said.

Mr. Bellows shook his head. "No. I put them out the day before yesterday. The only one who could have seen them was Mr. Darden. He was in right before I closed up for the evening that day. But I don't think he even noticed them. He was looking for a ring."

"Did anyone else know you had the rubies?" asked Jessie.

"Just me. And the woman who sold them to me, of course. Dr. Anne Marie Kroll," Mr. Bellows told them.

"Do you think Mr. Darden or Ms. Smitts might remember more about what happened?" Violet asked.

Straightening up, Mr. Bellows said, "I don't know. Ask them yourself if you'd like." He reached into his pocket and brought out his notebook. He flipped it open and tore out the piece of paper where they had written their names and addresses.

"Thanks!" Jessie said.

Outside the store, Henry said, "I think we should visit Mr. Darden first."

"Me, too," Jessie agreed. "I think it is suspicious that he hasn't come back to shop for a ring."

"And he didn't want the police to have his name and address, either," Violet reminded them. "That sounds suspicious, too."

"It sure does," Henry said. He looked at his watch. "I think we just have time to get supplies and pay a visit to Mr. Darden before lunch. He might be the key to the whole mystery!"

CHAPTER 5

An Empty Box and a Silver Star

Mr. Darden's house was on a quiet street not far from Main Street. The house had a small porch, and flowers grew in pots on either side of the front steps.

When he opened the door, Mr. Darden looked surprised. "What are you doing here?" he asked.

"We'd like to ask you a few more questions about the robbery at Antique Treasures," Henry said.

David Darden glanced over his shoulder, then quickly stepped out onto the porch, closing the door behind him. "What do you want to know?" he said.

"Do you know anyone named Marvin Map?" Jessie asked.

"No!" Mr. Darden said. He hesitated and then said, "Except what I read about him in the newspaper, of course."

"Why didn't you want to give your name and address to Mr. Bellows for the police?" Jessie went on.

Mr. Darden said, "Shhh, keep your voice down." He looked over his shoulder again.

"And why haven't you been back to buy a ring like you said you would?" Benny demanded.

"Shhh!" Mr. Darden said sharply. Then he said, "Will you please go away!" And without saying another word, he turned and went back inside, closing the door firmly behind him.

The Aldens were so surprised that they didn't speak for a moment. Then they turned and went back down the steps to their bicycles. Jessie glanced over her shoulder at the house as they rode away. "He's hiding something," she said. "And don't forget, he knew the rubies were there, or he could have known. The only other people were Mr. Bellows and Dr. Kroll."

After lunch, the Alden children gathered supplies to take out to the boxcar. They were going to work on the party decorations there.

But as they reached the boxcar, their steps slowed. Watch growled softly and the hair on his neck stood up.

"What is this?" Jessie asked.

"It looks like Benny's cereal," Violet said.

Benny ran forward. "It is!" he cried. "Someone has sprinkled Stars all over the ground."

The Aldens bent to examine the spilled cereal. Watch trotted around the corner of the boxcar. A moment later, he trotted back with something in his mouth. It was the empty cereal box.

"The thief must have dropped the box

while he was running away last night," said Henry. "Good dog, Watch." Watch cocked his head and panted.

Jessie looked puzzled. "But why did he open it before he dropped it?"

"Why did he take it if he didn't want to eat the cereal?" Violet wondered.

"Hmmm," said Jessie. "If you ask me, the cereal box mystery is even harder than the jewelry mystery — we know why someone would steal valuable jewelry. But why would anyone steal a box of cereal?"

When Soo Lee arrived, the Aldens told her what had happened. She was just as puzzled as they were. "But if we scatter the cereal in the grass," she said, "at least the birds can eat it."

"Good idea, Soo Lee," said Jessie.

Soo Lee and Violet and Benny scooped up the cereal that was spilled near the box-car and scattered it across the lawn for the birds. Watch helped by eating pieces of the cereal.

"Oh, Watch!" Soo Lee laughed. "You're a silly dog."

Watch wagged his tail.

"It's good cereal, isn't it, Watch?" asked Benny.

Watch wagged his tail again.

"I've never had any," said Soo Lee.

"You've never had Silver Frosted Stars?" Benny's eyes widened. "Wait right here."

He hurried away and returned with his opened box of cereal. Going into the boxcar, he returned with the old cracked pink cup that had been his when he and his sisters and brother had lived in the boxcar. He poured some of the cereal into the cup.

"Here," he said. "You can eat it without milk. We'll eat Stars while we make decorations for Grandfather's party."

The Aldens worked all afternoon. Benny and Soo Lee made a big poster that said HAPPY BIRTHDAY GRANDFATHER in bright letters. They painted a rainbow behind the words.

Violet painted a bouquet of purple flowers with green leaves and drew a frame around it for Grandfather Alden. Jessie and Henry gathered branches of greenery to make into birthday wreaths.

"We can pick flowers on his birthday and make a big birthday bouquet," said Jessie.

"We could paint pinecones different colors and put them in a big glass bowl," said Soo Lee. "That would be pretty."

"I know, I know! I know an even better idea," cried Benny, bouncing up and down in excitement.

"What is it, Benny?" asked Violet.

"We can get Grandfather a special tree and decorate it. Then we can plant it and he will have it forever and ever," Benny said.

"That's a terrific idea, Benny," said Jessie admiringly. "We'll put all our money together and go pick out a perfect tree tomorrow."

Violet suddenly turned her head and frowned.

"What is it, Violet?" asked Soo Lee.

"I don't know," said Violet. She looked around uneasily. Then she said, "I must be imagining things. But I just had the strangest feeling that someone was watching us."

The other Aldens looked around, too. But they couldn't see anyone.

Then Watch jumped up and raced toward the woods behind the house, barking as loudly as he could!

CHAPTER 6

A Spy in the Woods

"Watch, come back!" shouted Henry. He ran after Watch. So did all the others.

As they reached the edge of the woods, they heard crashing sounds and heavy footsteps. A shadowy figure ran between two big trees and then disappeared.

The Aldens ran after the figure. But they had to stop at a steep bank leading down to a wide stream. Watch ran up and down the bank, barking fiercely.

Jessie caught Watch. "Good boy," she said. "Good dog."

"You were right, Violet!" Soo Lee exclaimed. "Someone *was* watching us."

"But why?" asked Henry.

"It was the cereal box thief," said Benny. "He didn't find the silver star, so he came back to steal more cereal."

"Oh, Benny, that doesn't make sense. Why steal cereal when you can just buy it at the store?" asked Violet.

"I don't know," said Benny, looking stubborn.

"Here's another footprint," Jessie said suddenly. She pointed. Sure enough, in the mud at the very edge of the stream was a footprint. It wasn't very big.

"This isn't at all like the footprint we found by the front door," said Henry. "It's much smaller."

"That means there are two cereal thieves," said Benny.

"Maybe." But Henry didn't sound so sure. "Or maybe the footprint just looks smaller because of the mud. See? It's already filling up with water."

"Or maybe the thief wore extra-big boots last night as a disguise," Soo Lee suggested.

"That's possible, too," Henry agreed.

Jessie sighed. "We have a mystery and we have clues," she said. "But nothing makes any sense."

"Let's walk along the creek for a little ways," Henry said. "Maybe the spy crossed it again and we can follow the spy's tracks to find out who it is."

"Good idea," said Jessie.

They walked along the creek. A little while later, Soo Lee found another footprint. This footprint was small, just as the other one had been. And it was going up the side of the bank.

They raced into the woods — and stopped. No more footprints could be seen. Then Watch growled softly.

"Can you smell the person?" asked Benny. "Can you find who it is and where he went?"

As if he understood Benny, Watch ran

forward. They followed him through the woods. Without warning, they crashed out of the trees — and into their own backyard.

Watch ran up to the boxcar and barked loudly.

"He's trapped the spy in our boxcar!" cried Benny. He ran up to the boxcar, put his hands around his mouth, and said, "Come out and surrender! We have you surrounded!"

The Aldens waited with their hearts pounding. But no one came out of the boxcar.

"I don't think anyone is in there," Violet whispered to Soo Lee.

"Me neither," Soo Lee whispered back.

"If you don't come out," said Jessie loudly, "we're coming in."

No one answered.

Slowly they walked up to the boxcar. Cautiously, they peered inside.

It was empty.

Then Violet's eyes widened. She raised her hands to her cheeks. "Oh, Benny," she gasped. "You were right. Whoever it was stole your box of cereal!"

Sure enough, the box of cereal that Benny had brought out to the boxcar was missing. All that was left of it was the cereal in the cracked pink cup.

"And look," said Henry. "There is a fresh smear of mud on the stump that we use as a step into the boxcar. Our thief must have stood here to reach inside and grab the cereal."

"So someone was watching us so that he could steal Benny's box of cereal?" Violet looked down at the pink ring on her finger and rubbed it absently. "It just doesn't make sense."

"Maybe Mr. Map is trying to steal my Silver Frosted Stars for the prizes inside," said Benny. "Violet and Jessie both got rings."

"No, Benny," Jessie said. She held out her hand. "The green stone in my ring is pretty, but it isn't a real emerald."

"I think my pink ring is pretty, too," said Violet. "But I don't think a thief would want it."

"But who did take the real jewels?" Benny said.

"And where did he put them?" Soo Lee added.

"Remember, the gift shop owner said that Marvin Map almost looked as if he wanted the police to catch him," Henry said. "Maybe he did. Maybe he was just trying to distract them while an accomplice stole the jewels."

"An accomplice like Mr. Darden. He was acting awfully suspiciously this morning," Jessie said.

"Yes," Henry agreed. "Tomorrow, we're going to follow Mr. Darden and see what he is up to."

That night, Watch lifted his head and growled softly. Benny woke up.

"What is it, boy? Is it another burglar?" Watch growled again, but he didn't jump off the bed or bark.

Benny listened with all his might, but he couldn't hear anything at all. After a while, Watch lowered his head.

"Good boy," Benny whispered, petting Watch. "Don't worry. I brought the cereal with me. It's on the top shelf of my closet and I'm going to keep it there until breakfast tomorrow. No one will think of looking for it there."

Watch's tail thumped slightly, as if he understood. Then he and Benny went back to sleep.

CHAPTER 7

Too Many Rings!

"I don't believe this!" Mrs. Mc-Gregor said.

"What?" asked Henry, coming into the kitchen the next morning, followed by Benny, Jessie, Violet, and Watch.

"Take a look outside the back door," Mrs. McGregor said. "Some animal got into the garbage and turned it over last night. Some dog, probably."

She glanced at Watch. Benny said, "Watch stayed with me last night!"

Mrs. McGregor smiled. "I know Watch

would never do such a thing," she said.

"We'll clean it up," Henry said.

The Aldens went outside. As they began to pick up the garbage, Violet said, "That's strange."

"What?" Jessie asked.

"There are chicken bones in the garbage," Violet said. "If a dog or any other animal had turned over the can, wouldn't the bones have been eaten?"

"Yes," Henry said. Then he said, "You know, it does look as if a person — not a dog — was going through the garbage."

It was true. The contents of the can weren't scattered all over the yard, but spread out neatly.

"You're right, Henry!" Jessie exclaimed. "Someone did go through our garbage last night."

"Watch growled last night while I was asleep. I woke up, but he stopped growling. He must have heard the garbage can being turned over," Benny said.

"But what was the person looking for?" Violet asked.

"I don't know, Violet," Henry answered. "It's a mystery, that's for sure."

Just as they finished cleaning up the mess, Soo Lee rode up on her bicycle. "Hi," she said. "I got here as early as I could. Are you ready to go follow Mr. Darden?"

"Yes, and we'd better hurry," Jessie agreed.

The Aldens got on their bicycles and rode to David Darden's small, tidy house on the edge of town. There they spotted some tall bushes to hide behind.

Soon Mr. Darden came out. He got in his car and drove toward Greenfield. The Aldens pedaled after him as fast as they could.

On Main Street, Mr. Darden got out and parked his car near the town square. He walked briskly down the street. The Aldens walked after him. When he stopped, they stopped and pretended to be looking in store windows.

They followed Mr. Darden to a jewelry store.

Violet gasped and grabbed Jessie's arm.

"You don't think he's planning another robbery, do you?"

"I don't think so, but maybe he is," Jessie answered. She looked up and down the street, half expecting to see a man with a hat pulled low and wearing a tan raincoat. But she saw no one like that.

"Should we call the police?" Benny asked.

"Let's just keep an eye on him for now," Jessie said.

They walked past the window of the jewelry store. They could see Mr. Darden in the back, bent over a glass counter. All around the walls of the jewelry store, rings and necklaces and bracelets glittered and gleamed.

"We should go in and see what he is up to," Violet whispered, as if she were afraid Mr. Darden could hear her.

"We can't all go in," Henry said. "But I think some of us should."

"You and I could go in, Violet," Jessie said. "We could pretend we're looking for a gift for Grandfather's birthday."

"Yes, and we'll wait out here to stop him if something happens," said Benny.

Violet and Jessie walked into the jewelry store. They stood at a counter near Mr. Darden. "Look at the pocket watches," Jessie said. "Maybe Grandfather would like one of those."

"But he already has a pocket watch," Violet said. Jessie nudged her.

"Oh," said Violet. "Yes. The pocket watches are nice."

Watching Mr. Darden and one of the jewelers out of the corner of her eye, Jessie saw the jeweler hand Mr. Darden a small box. Mr. Darden opened it.

What was inside? Jessie couldn't see.

With a little gasp, Violet grabbed Jessie's arm.

"What? What is it?" Jessie asked.

"I thought I saw someone go by the window," Violet said.

"Who?" Jessie asked.

"The man in the tan raincoat," Violet said. "Maybe he's about to come in and rob the place."

They waited tensely as Mr. Darden closed the small box and put it in his pocket. He thanked the jeweler and walked out.

Both Violet and Jessie let out a sigh of relief. "I guess he wasn't going to rob the store after all," Jessie said, forgetting to lower her voice.

The jeweler heard her and gave her a funny look, but Jessie didn't notice as she and Violet hurried out the door to join the others.

"There goes Mr. Darden," Henry said. "Come on."

They followed Mr. Darden down the street to the town square. He stopped once and peered into a store window, smoothing his hair and adjusting his tie.

"What's he doing?" Benny asked.

"He's using the window as a mirror," Jessie said.

When he'd finished, Mr. Darden patted his pocket. Then he smiled and walked toward a bench by a flower bed.

They saw a young woman stand up and smile at Mr. Darden. Then the couple sat down on the bench and began to talk. Suddenly Mr. Darden took the small box from his pocket. He got down on one knee, opened the box, and handed it to the woman. She put her hands to her cheeks and looked very surprised and happy.

"That must be Mr. Darden's girlfriend," Violet said. "It's *so* romantic."

"What if the ring he is giving her is the stolen ring?" Jessie asked.

"Come on," Henry said, and led the way toward the bench.

The young woman was holding up her hand now, admiring the ring. Mr. Darden had gotten up to sit next to her again.

"Hi," Benny said.

Mr. Darden looked up, startled. "You again!" he said.

"Is that the ring you were shopping for at Antique Treasures?" Jessie asked bluntly.

"No," Mr. Darden said. Then he smiled. "I bought the ring at a different store."

"What kind of ring is it?" Benny asked. "Is it a ruby?"

The young woman laughed. "Oh, no," she said. "It's an emerald."

Jessie glanced down at the green ring on her own finger. "Like this?" she said.

The young woman held out her hand. On it was a slender gold band with a small yellow stone in the center.

"That's not an emerald," Jessie said. "Emeralds are green."

But Mr. Darden was shaking his head. "Not all emeralds. They come in different colors. So do rubies and diamonds and many precious gems — you can even find black diamonds."

The woman said, "I think this is the most beautiful emerald in the world."

Mr. Darden said, "I wanted to ask you yesterday when I made lunch for you, Janie, but I was too nervous. And this ring wasn't ready yet."

"Now I know why you weren't hungry!" Janie said.

"You were at Mr. Darden's yesterday?" Violet asked Janie.

She nodded, her gaze still on her engagement ring. "We're engaged to be married now."

Mr. Darden said to the Aldens, "I'm sorry if I seemed distracted when you came to visit. But I didn't want Janie to hear you talking about a ring. I was afraid it would spoil the surprise."

"Was that why you told Mr. Bellows you didn't want your name in the newspaper?" Jessie asked.

"Yes. I was afraid Janie might see it and somehow guess what I was planning," Mr. Darden said.

Janie smiled at Mr. Darden. Mr. Darden smiled back.

"We have to go," Jessie said. "Congratulations."

The newly engaged couple didn't even look at the Aldens as they left. "Good-bye," said Mr. Darden absently.

As they walked their bikes away, Jessie said, "That explains why Mr. Darden was acting so strangely."

With a laugh, Henry said, "It sure does."

"If Mr. Darden didn't help Mr. Map, then maybe Ms. Smitts did," Violet said.

Jessie reached in her pocket and took out

the piece of paper with the names and addresses of Mr. Darden and Ms. Smitts on them. She said, "Ms. Smitts didn't leave an address, only a phone number."

"We can call her from the phone booth on the corner, then," Henry said.

When they called, a voice said, "Karate Center." Surprised, Henry said hesitantly, "May I please speak to Ms. Tori Smitts?"

"She's not available right now," the voice said. "May I take a message?"

"I'm Henry Alden. We wanted to talk to her for a few minutes."

"Ms. Smitts should be free in just about fifteen minutes," the receptionist said.

"Could we have your address?" Henry asked. "We could come by."

He wrote down the address and hung up the phone. The Aldens pedaled to the Karate Center, which wasn't far from Main Street.

Inside, a young man behind a battered desk was typing something into a small computer. On a shelf behind him was a row of trophies.

"Excuse me," Jessie said. "We called a few minutes ago. We'd like to speak to Ms. Smitts."

The young man looked up and pointed. "She's in the studio," he said. "You can sit on that bench and watch through the glass, if you'd like. She'll be out soon."

"Did you win all those trophies?" Benny asked.

"Those?" The young man glanced over his shoulder. "Not yet. I still have a lot to learn. No, those trophies belong to our instructors. They've all earned their black belts. That means they're the best."

"Oh," said Benny. He sat down next to the others. They watched as Tori Smitts, in loose white pants and a white coat, wearing a black belt, showed students how to kick and punch and block.

Sometimes the students tried to knock her down. No matter how hard they tried, she always won.

"She's very good," Jessie said admiringly.

"Oh, yes," the young man said. "Practically unbeatable."

A few minutes later, they heard Ms. Smitts say, "Okay, that's it."

Everyone bowed. Then the students filed out through a door in the back of the studio that had the words LOCKER ROOMS on it.

The young man got up, tapped on the glass, and motioned to Ms. Smitts. She walked toward him, then opened the door and stepped into the reception area.

"You have some visitors," the receptionist said.

The Aldens stood up. "Hello," Henry said, and began to introduce everyone.

Ms. Smitts looked surprised. But she held up her hand. "I remember you," she said. "You don't need to introduce yourselves. And I bet I can solve a mystery."

"What?" asked Benny. "What mystery?"

"The mystery of why you're here," she said. Her lips curled into a little smile. "You're playing detective, right? You're looking for the missing jewelry."

"And the thief," said Benny. He wasn't sure, but he thought Ms. Smitts might be teasing him and the other Aldens. He stared at her hard.

"We just wondered if you could remember anything else about what happened — anything that might be helpful," Violet said.

"I've told the police everything I know," Ms. Smitts said. "It all happened so fast."

"So even though you grabbed the thief just outside the front door, you didn't see his face," Henry suggested.

"He pushed me away so hard, I nearly fell. I wasn't able to hold on to him, much less see what he looked like," Ms. Smitts replied firmly. "Now, if that's all, I have another class to teach. Good luck to you."

She turned and walked away.

The Aldens left, feeling discouraged.

"She wasn't very friendly," Violet said. "But I guess that doesn't mean she is hiding anything."

"Besides, she tried to keep the thief from getting away. That was very brave," Jessie said. She paused, then added, "Unless she was just pretending, to keep people from being suspicious."

"But she couldn't have taken the jewelry after the thief left," Henry pointed out. "Mr. Darden was still in the shop."

"Maybe they were all three working together," Jessie said.

"Maybe," said Henry. "But I don't think so."

"I don't, either," said Violet. "I don't think Mr. Darden had anything to do with it."

"Maybe the thief dropped the jewelry in some special place and whoever was helping him picked it up afterward," Jessie said.

"That could have happened," Henry said.

"But Ms. Smitts walked away in the opposite direction from where the thief had gone," Violet pointed out. "And Mr. Darden stayed on Main Street, looking in shop windows."

"We still have two suspects," Henry said.

"Who?" asked Benny.

"Mr. Bellows," Henry began.

"But why would Mr. Bellows steal his own jewelry from himself?" Benny cried.

"I don't know, Benny. But I think we

should go talk to him and find out," Henry said.

"Who's the other suspect?" Jessie asked.

"Dr. Kroll," said Henry.

"Of course!" Jessie said. "She knew Mr. Bellows had the necklace. Why, she could have sold the necklace to Mr. Bellows — and then stolen it back."

"Mr. Bellows could even have helped her," Henry said. "C'mon, let's go talk to Mr. Bellows right now."

CHAPTER 8

A Birthday Present and a Clue

Mr. Bellows was sitting behind his counter. He looked as if he hadn't moved since the last time they had spoken to him. Only a single lamp burned in the shop. It was dark and gloomy.

When the Aldens came in, he looked up. For a moment, he looked hopeful. "Have you heard anything about the jewelry?" he asked.

Shaking her head, Jessie said, "No. I'm sorry."

Mr. Bellows's shoulders slumped forward.

"That's okay," he mumbled, resting his head on his hands again.

"Mr. Bellows," Henry said, "didn't you have insurance for such valuable jewelry?"

Still staring down at nothing, Mr. Bellows said, "I have insurance for everything in my shop. But I had just gotten the necklace set and I hadn't gotten extra insurance. I couldn't afford it just yet. I had to borrow money to buy it. Of course, I hoped to sell it for much more."

"Does that mean that the insurance won't pay for it?" Violet asked.

Mr. Bellows shook his head mournfully. "Not even as much as I borrowed to buy the necklace, bracelet, and ring," he said. "Oh, why wasn't I more careful? Why did I even have it out on display? A perfect matched set of cabochon rubies. Oh, dear. Oh, dear."

Violet said, "What about Dr. Kroll?"

Mr. Bellows took off his glasses and wiped them with a tissue. He peered shortsightedly at Violet. "What about Dr. Kroll?" he repeated.

"She knew you had the rubies — could she have stolen them back?" Henry asked boldly.

"Dr. Kroll?" asked Mr. Bellows. "Oh, no. That wasn't Dr. Kroll who ran out of here with the necklace set. She is six feet tall and has bright red hair. I would have recognized Dr. Kroll immediately."

"Oh," Jessie said, disappointed.

Mr. Bellows put his glasses on and stared back down at the glass countertop.

"Don't worry," Benny told him. "We'll find your rubies."

The shop owner glanced up and tried to smile. But it wasn't much of a smile. He looked back down again. "I wish you could," he said.

At the door of the shop, Violet turned. "Mr. Bellows," she said, "what are cab . . . cab . . ."

"Cabochon rubies?" Mr. Bellows looked up for a moment, staring into space. He said, "Cabochon just means rounded, sort of like a marble. Most jewels are cut into square surfaces called facets before they are polished. But cabochon jewels are cut round and then polished. When gemstones are cut into facets, they sparkle more. Cabochons don't sparkle as much. But they are still beautiful."

"Oh," Violet said. "Thank you."

Mr. Bellows didn't answer. He had rested his head in his hands again, staring down at nothing.

"Wow," Jessie said after they had left the store. "Either Mr. Bellows is a really good actor or he didn't have anything to do with the theft."

"He could be lying about not having enough insurance," Henry said.

"And about Dr. Kroll?" asked Benny.

"No. No, because Mr. Darden and Ms. Smitts would have remembered someone who was really tall, too," said Jessie. "I guess that means Dr. Kroll didn't steal her jewels back."

"I don't think Mr. Bellows did it, either," Violet said, shaking her head.

"If Mr. Map doesn't have the rubies, and

Mr. Darden doesn't have them, and Ms. Smitts doesn't have them, and Mr. Bellows doesn't have them, and Dr. Kroll doesn't have them, then who does?" Benny demanded.

"I don't know, Benny." Jessie frowned. "It's almost as if they have disappeared into thin air."

That afternoon, the Aldens decided to go pick out a tree for Grandfather's birthday.

"Here. 'Greenfield Nursery, Plant and Tree Specialists,' " Violet read aloud from the phone book.

"That sounds like the perfect place," Jessie said.

As they rode their bikes to the Greenfield Nursery on the other side of town, they talked about all the mysterious events.

"You don't think that whoever is following us and stealing boxes of cereal has anything to do with the jewelry theft, do you?" asked Violet.

Jessie shook her head. "Nooo . . . but I guess it's possible. After all, everything that happened to us happened after the jewelry store robbery."

"Maybe the thief thinks we saw something and is trying to find out what it is," Henry suggested.

"But what? We didn't even see what the thief looked like when he ran by," Jessie said.

They pulled their bikes to a stop outside the nursery and parked them.

Inside, an older woman with curly dark hair streaked with gray and friendly brown eyes came up to them. She was wearing blue overalls with the words GREENFIELD NURSERY embroidered across the front. "Hello," she said. "I'm Adella. Welcome to the Greenfield Nursery. May I help you?"

"We're here to buy a tree," Benny said. "It's a birthday present for Grandfather."

"What a good idea for a present," said the woman, the corners of her eyes crinkling in a smile. "What kind of tree did you have in mind?"

"A beautiful one," said Violet.

The woman smiled more broadly. "I think all trees are beautiful," she said. "But if you'll follow me, I'll show you some that I think you might like."

The Aldens followed Adella through the nursery. Adella showed them several trees, including one called a Japanese maple with beautiful red leaves. "It looks like it is made of rubies when the sun shines through it," she said. "Most maple trees have leaves that turn beautiful colors in the fall, but this one has beautiful red leaves spring, summer, and fall."

"Like rubies," said Violet softly. She touched one of the leaves gently.

"I like this Christmas tree over here," said Benny.

"It's a lovely tree," Adella agreed. "It's called a blue spruce. That would make a good gift, too. Why don't you look around and then you can ask me questions if you have any. I'll be at the counter."

"Thank you," said Henry.

The Aldens looked at all kinds of trees,

short, tall, fat, thin, with needles, and with leaves. But at last they decided on the tree with the ruby-colored leaves.

"I think Grandfather will really like his birthday tree," said Jessie as they walked to the counter to pay for the Japanese maple and arrange for it to be delivered. They decided to plant it in the backyard near the boxcar.

"We can have the surprise party there, too," said Jessie. "That way we can decorate and Grandfather won't know."

As they were leaving, Violet stopped by a small plant. "That looks like a violet, but it has pink flowers," she said. She smiled shyly at Adella. "That's my name, Violet."

Adella smiled back. "Violets come in a variety of colors. I've been experimenting, too, trying to get some new colors. I call that violet Ruby Pink."

"Ruby Pink," Violet said. "It's beautiful." She reached out and touched the pot as if she were petting the plant.

"Violet," Jessie cried. "Your hand! It's on your hand! Don't move!"

Violet froze. "Is it a spider?" she asked.

"No," Jessie said. "It's your ring."

She looked at Adella. The greenhouse owner said, "Why, it's the same color as the ruby pink violet."

"It is!" Benny said.

"It's a pretty ring," Adella said. "It looks old."

"It is," Jessie said, to everyone's surprise. "It's an antique. Thank you for your help. We have to go."

Jessie grabbed Violet's hand and led the way out of the Greenfield Nursery.

Outside, she stopped. "Look at your ring, Violet," Jessie commanded.

Violet looked down at the pink ring that had come out of Benny's cereal box. The stone was dark pink and rounded, polished like a marble. The setting was fancy and old-fashioned-looking.

With a little gasp, Henry said, "Emeralds come in different colors. And *rubies* come in different colors. . . ."

"Like ruby pink," Jessie said.

"And cabochon stones are round and polished, like marbles," Henry said.

"Like Violet's ring," Benny almost shouted.

"Shhh, Benny!" Jessie said.

Then they all stared down at the ring on Violet's hand. Violet said wonderingly, "Is that why my ring is so heavy? Because it is *real*?"

"I think so, Violet," Henry said.

"But how did the stolen ring get into my cereal box?" asked Benny.

"The thief must have put it there," Jessie said. "Remember how your bike was turned over and everything was spilled out, Benny?"

Benny nodded.

"The thief must have run into your bike and slipped the ring inside the open box of cereal," Jessie said.

"And the thief thinks that the ring is still in the cereal box!" exclaimed Violet. "That's why he's been watching us."

"Yes," Henry said. "And that's why he

broke into our house and stole the cereal."

"And went through our garbage," Jessie said.

"He stole the cereal from our boxcar, too," Benny said. "He's a cereal thief and a jewelry thief."

"But where is the rest of the jewelry?" Violet asked.

Henry said, "I'm not sure. It's not in our empty cereal box, that's for sure. But I have an idea. Let's go visit Mr. Bellows one more time."

Inside Antique Treasures, Violet walked up to the counter. She held out her hand. "Mr. Bellows," she said. "I think we found something that belongs to you."

For a moment, Mr. Bellows stared down at Violet's hand. Then he leaped to his feet. He looked as if he were about to start dancing. His mouth opened and closed, but no words came out. "The ring," he managed to say at last. "The cabochon ring! Where did you find it?"

"In *my* cereal box," Benny answered.

"But how did it get there? When? I don't

understand," Mr. Bellows said. He took a handkerchief out of his pocket and mopped his forehead. "Where is the necklace? And the bracelet?"

Henry said, "We're not sure. But can you tell us one thing? When the thief ran out of the shop, was Ms. Smitts by the door?"

After thinking for a moment, Mr. Bellows shook his head. "No. She was standing near the counter."

"That means she ran all the way across the shop and out the door after him," Jessie said. "He had a pretty big head start, but she caught up with him right outside the door."

"That's right," Mr. Bellows said. "It was a brave thing for her to do. She could have been hurt when the thief pushed her. As it was, her shirt got torn."

But Henry was shaking his head. "It doesn't make sense," he said. "Ms. Smitts should never have been able to catch up with the thief. When she did, though, she should have been able to stop him."

"I don't understand," Mr. Bellows said.

He looked more puzzled than ever.

Jessie burst out, "Ms. Smitts teaches karate. In fact, she has a black belt in karate. That means she's really, really good."

"With a black belt in karate, she should have been able to at least stop the thief for a minute. Instead, he pushed her away and kept running," Violet said.

Benny was looking from one to the other, his eyes round. He said, "Why did Ms. Smitts let the thief go, then?"

"Because they were partners, Benny. They were working together," Henry said.

Now Mr. Bellows was nodding. "It makes sense. She stood in front of me by the counter, blocking my view of the glass case where the necklace set was. She got in front of me when I shouted for the thief to stop —"

"And she pretended to go after the thief so you wouldn't be suspicious," Violet said.

"Oh, it was more than that, Violet," Jessie said. She glanced at Henry and smiled. "Much more than that."

"But how do we prove any of this?" Mr.

Bellows said. "I'm glad you found the ring, but it is much more valuable when it is part of the set."

"I know how we can find the necklace and the bracelet — and catch the thief," Henry said. He looked at Violet's hand, which was still resting on the top of the glass case. "We'll set a trap. But we'll have to use the cabochon ring as bait."

Mr. Bellows stared down at the ring. Then he looked back up at the Aldens. Slowly he nodded. "Let's do it," he said. "Let's set a trap and catch the thief."

CHAPTER 9

A Picnic Surprise

"What a great day for a picnic," Henry said. "Look, there's a good place, right there near the trees." He parked his bike and took a blanket out of the basket. He and Violet spread the blanket out on the ground.

Jessie unstrapped a picnic basket from the back of her bicycle and put it on the blanket. She opened it and took out knives, forks, spoons, plates, cups, and napkins.

"I'm hungry," Benny said. "I hope we brought lots and lots of food."

"Don't worry, Benny, we have plenty," Violet assured him. She unloaded sandwiches and fruit and some of Mrs. McGregor's homemade cookies from the picnic basket.

"Just in case, I brought another box of cereal," Benny said. "It's a good thing we got all those boxes of cereal when we went to the grocery store the other day."

"Oh, Benny." Jessie laughed. "Won't you ever get tired of eating Silver Frosted Stars?"

"No," said Benny. "It's the best cereal in the whole world. And in this box, maybe there'll be another silver star. I only need one more to send away for the special detective's badge."

He put the cereal next to him on the grass.

Watch sat down next to Henry, keeping a close eye on the sandwiches. Watch liked peanut butter.

Soo Lee said, "When is the tree being delivered for Grandfather's party?"

"This afternoon," Henry said. "Grandfather is going to be in Silver City, so he won't see it arrive."

"We can get up early tomorrow morning and make a few more decorations for the tree," Violet said. "Before we start getting ready for the party."

"You don't think Mrs. McGregor will forget to make the birthday cake, do you?" Benny asked anxiously.

Henry laughed. "No, Benny, Mrs. McGregor won't forget the cake. Don't worry. Have a sandwich."

But Benny shook his head. "I'm going to open my new box of cereal," he announced. He opened the box, got a cup, and poured out some cereal.

He stopped and stared into the cup.

"What is it, Benny? What's wrong?" asked Soo Lee.

"Look!" Benny said. "Look at the prize that came in my cereal."

He reached into his cup and pulled out the pink cabochon ruby ring.

"Oh, Benny, it's a ring. A pink ring!" Violet cried.

"It's beautiful," Jessie said loudly. "What a great prize to find in a box of cereal!"

At that moment Watch growled. Henry grabbed Watch's leash and held on tightly.

"Let me see the ring, Benny," Jessie said. Benny handed his oldest sister the ring. She held it up high, so high that anyone in the park who was looking could see it.

Suddenly a voice said, "Well, well, well, if it isn't the Aldens."

Startled, Jessie looked up, almost dropping the ring. "Ms. Smitts!" she gasped.

"What are you doing in the park?" Ms. Smitts asked. She smiled.

"We're having a picnic," Benny said. "I'm having cereal. Look at the prize I found in the cereal box."

Ms. Smitts focused on the ring. Her eyes narrowed. Then she smiled again. "What a cute toy ring," she said.

"It's a ruby ring," Benny said.

Henry gave Benny a warning look. Ms. Smitts laughed. "What a good imagination you have, Benny, to be able to pretend that a pink plastic ring is a real ruby."

Now Ms. Smitts was speaking in a loud voice, too.

Then everything seemed to happen at once. Watch leaped forward to the end of his leash and began to bark. Someone burst out of the woods and pushed Jessie over, snatching the ring from her hand.

"Stop, thief!" Henry cried.

The thief ran right across the picnic blanket, kicking aside the picnic basket. The Aldens had a glimpse of someone in a tan raincoat, with a hat pulled low on his forehead.

"Stop!" cried Ms. Smitts. She grabbed the thief by the arm. He pushed her and the two struggled for just a moment. Then Ms. Smitts let go and fell down. The thief began to run.

As he did, police officers surrounded the picnic. Two of them grabbed the thief by each arm. Two more officers grabbed Ms. Smitts and helped her to her feet. And Mr. Bellows ran out to stand by the picnic blanket.

"Thank you," said Ms. Smitts.

She tried to pull her arms free, but the officers held on.

"Let go," she said. "Let me go!" She began to struggle.

The Boxcar Children and Soo Lee and Watch got up and walked over to Ms. Smitts. She stopped struggling and glared at everyone. "Why are you treating me this way?" she demanded. "Is this the thanks I get for trying to prevent a robbery?"

"No," Jessie said. "That's not it. You won't get away with it this time, Ms. Smitts. We know you have the ruby ring. Give it back."

CHAPTER 10

A Special Badge for a Real Detective

"That's crazy!" Tori Smitts cried, pulling against the police officers who were holding her.

One of the police officers shook her head. "I'm afraid it isn't, Ms. Smitts. We expected your partner, Mr. Map, to slip the ring to you when you grabbed him this time. We saw it happen."

"It worked the first time," Mr. Bellows said. "But it won't work now."

Seeing Mr. Bellows, Ms. Smitts's eyes widened.

The other officers led the thief over to the others. His hat was gone and the handkerchief covering his face had been pulled around his neck. He was a pale man with piercing gray eyes and a thin, pointed chin.

"Meet Marvin Map," the police officer said.

"I told you it wouldn't work a second time, Marvin," Ms. Smitts gasped.

"Be quiet," Mr. Map ordered.

"We know you have the ring," Benny said to Ms. Smitts. "You should give it back. And the necklace and the bracelet."

"It wasn't my idea," said Ms. Smitts.

Mr. Map gave Ms. Smitts a disgusted look. "I don't have the ring," he said. "She does. She has the necklace and the bracelet, too."

Ms. Smitts and Mr. Map glared at one another for a moment. Then Ms. Smitts reached into her pocket and pulled out the ruby ring. She put it into Mr. Bellows's outstretched hand.

"The necklace and the bracelet are at my

house," she said. "In the back of a drawer in the basement."

"Mr. Map gave you the necklace and the bracelet when he ran out of the antique shop, didn't he?" Jessie asked.

Ms. Smitts nodded. "I managed to keep the lock on the glass case from snapping shut after Mr. Bellows showed the necklace set to Mr. Darden. That's how Marvin got it out of the glass case so fast. But he didn't have time to give me the ring. Mr. Bellows ran up behind me and I saw a police officer coming. Marvin had to run. When he did, he crashed into the bicycle. I saw him slip the ring into a box of cereal."

"It should have been safe there," Mr. Map growled.

"I tried to get it back right away," Ms. Smitts went on. "But you wouldn't throw the open box of cereal away."

"Who broke into our house and stole a box of cereal?" Benny asked, looking from Mr. Map to Ms. Smitts.

"That was me," Mr. Map admitted. "But

the dog started barking, so I just grabbed a box of cereal and ran."

Watch growled softly, as if remembering what had happened.

"You left footprints when you knocked over a flowerpot," Jessie said.

"You dumped the cereal out by the boxcar," Henry said.

Mr. Map nodded. "It was useless. The ring wasn't in there. I remembered seeing other boxes of cereal when I ran into the bike. I figured I must have gotten the wrong box of cereal."

"So you came back and saw us with the cereal when we were in the boxcar," Violet said. "I *felt* someone watching us." She shuddered at the memory.

"No, that was me," said Ms. Smitts.

"*That's* why the footprint we found by the stream was so much smaller," Jessie said. "You made it."

Nodding, Ms. Smitts said, "I doubled back to the boxcar and grabbed the cereal. But the ring wasn't in that box, either."

"We figured you hadn't found it yet, or

you would have realized what it was and gone to the police," Mr. Map put in. "So I went back that night to check your garbage." He made a disgusted face. "Nothing!"

"We didn't know what else to do," Ms. Smitts added, "so we started following you. And today you found the ring in the cereal box."

"But we didn't," Henry said. "We found the ring the very first day."

"You did?" Ms. Smitts said.

"Yes. We didn't know it was a ruby ring. Benny gave it to Violet. She was wearing it when we went to visit you at the Karate Center," Jessie explained.

"Oh, no! You mean this was all a trick?" cried Ms. Smitts.

"Yes," Henry said. "When we realized that we had the ring and how it got into the cereal box, we set a trap using a new box of cereal — and the police."

"See?" Benny said. "We did solve the mystery after all."

"It was a dirty trick!" Mr. Map shouted. "Sneaky."

"No, it wasn't. What was sneaky was stealing the jewelry from Mr. Bellows," Henry said.

"That's right," Benny added. "You were wrong. Stealing is wrong."

"Mr. Map, Ms. Smitts, my advice to you is that you listen to what Benny Alden just said. It might keep you out of trouble in the future. Let's go," one of the officers said.

The police led the two thieves away.

"I have to go with the police," Mr. Bellows said. "To identify the necklace and the bracelet." He took a small box out of his pocket and carefully put the ring inside. "How can I ever thank you?"

"We're glad we could help," Henry said.

Mr. Bellows shook hands with Henry, Jessie, Violet, and Soo Lee. But when he got to Benny, Benny dropped to his knees. "Look!" he said. He picked something up from the cereal that had spilled across the picnic blanket.

It was a small silver cardboard star.

"It's the last star," Benny said happily.

"Now I can send away for my detective's badge!"

The next day was Grandfather's birthday. But Violet and Benny had one thing to do before helping with the preparations.

"Hurry," Violet said. "We haven't got much time."

"Here's the mailbox," Benny said. He opened it and dropped the envelope inside. He peered through the opening to make sure the letter had gone in. It was addressed to the cereal company. Inside were all the silver stars that Benny needed to get his detective's badge.

They walked home quickly from the mailbox on the corner and hurried around to the boxcar.

Inside, Jessie was spreading a tablecloth across the old table. In the middle of it, she put a vase with flowers that she had picked that day. Outside, Soo Lee was hanging pinecones coated with glitter and paint and tied to ribbons on a small red maple tree near the boxcar. Benny ran to help her.

"Violet, would you hand me the tape, please?" Henry asked. "I dropped it."

Violet hurried to pick up the tape and hand it to her brother. He taped the corner of the poster above the door. It said, HAPPY BIRTHDAY GRANDFATHER.

At that moment, Mrs. McGregor came out the back door. In her hands she held a beautiful cake, with pink and lavender roses and green leaves made of sugar. On top of the cake were blue candles.

"That is the best birthday cake I've ever seen," Violet said, clasping her hands together.

"And the most delicious one you'll ever eat," Mrs. McGregor assured her. "Until my next one. Now, who wants to help me bring out the punch?"

"I will," said Benny. He skipped alongside Mrs. McGregor as she went back to the house. "I could lick the frosting bowl for you," he volunteered.

Mrs. McGregor laughed.

Henry looked at his watch. "Cousin Alice and Cousin Joe will be here in ten minutes," he said.

They all worked faster than ever. At last Violet tied a big bow on the Japanese maple tree.

A car pulled into the driveway.

Quickly everyone jumped into the boxcar and pulled the door closed.

Peering through a crack, they saw the back door open. Then they saw Mrs. McGregor gesture toward the boxcar.

"Do you think he suspects anything?" Jessie whispered.

"Not yet," said Henry. He held on to Benny to keep him from jumping out of the boxcar too early. Benny held on to Watch.

Grandfather, Mrs. McGregor, Alice, and Joe walked toward the boxcar.

"Now!" whispered Henry.

Jessie pushed open the boxcar door and they all leaped out.

"Surprise!" they all shouted, and Watch barked loudly.

Then, as Mrs. McGregor, Alice, and Joe joined in, they all began to sing "Happy Birthday."

Grandfather's mouth dropped open in

surprise. But when everyone had finished singing, he began to laugh.

"Are you surprised, Grandfather?" Benny asked.

"I sure am," his grandfather answered. He looked at Joe and Alice. "Did you know about this?"

Joe and Alice nodded. Alice said, "That's why we invited you to come visit — so there would be time to decorate the boxcar."

Benny said, "Do you want some cake? Mrs. McGregor made it. It's your favorite kind." He paused and added, "Mine, too."

Laughing, everybody went into the boxcar. Grandfather Alden blew out the candles on his cake. He cut it and gave everybody a piece, while Henry and Jessie poured the punch and Violet passed out the napkins.

"Let's eat our cake and drink our punch outside under a tree," Jessie said.

"Yes," Violet agreed. "I know just the tree."

"Come on, Grandfather," Benny said.

When they reached the tree, Grandfather said, "My goodness! Another surprise!"

"It's a Japanese maple tree," Henry said. "We picked it out ourselves."

"It's a wonderful tree. And it has some very fine decorations," Grandfather said.

"We made those," Soo Lee told him.

They sat down in the grass under the new tree and ate their cake and drank punch. Mrs. McGregor gave Watch a special dog biscuit that she had saved for the birthday celebration.

"With the sun shining through the red leaves of this maple, they are the color of rubies," Grandfather declared, looking up at his birthday tree.

"Some rubies," Violet said. "Not all rubies are red."

"Speaking of rubies," said Joe, "Alice and I have something to show you."

Alice reached into her shoulder bag and pulled out the latest edition of the Greenfield newspaper. "Your names are on page one," she told the Boxcar Children.

Sure enough, the newspaper had printed the whole story of the stolen jewels and how Henry, Jessie, Violet, Benny, and Soo

Lee had helped find and capture the robbers. The story even mentioned Watch.

"We'll have to save this," Henry said.

Benny sighed.

"What's wrong, Benny?" asked Violet.

"I wish I had my detective's badge," Benny said. "I could have worn it when we solved the case. Then I would have been a real detective."

Jessie laughed. "Oh, Benny. You don't need a detective's badge to be a real detective. You are one already."

"Really?" asked Benny.

"Yes!" declared Jessie.

"Not only are you all real detectives," said Grandfather Alden, looking around, "but you are my favorite detectives in the whole world. You are the very best."

"Is that true?" Benny asked.

"It certainly is, Benny," Grandfather said. "It certainly is."

GERTRUDE CHANDLER WARNER discovered when she was teaching that many readers who like an exciting story could find no books that were both easy and fun to read. She decided to try to meet this need, and her first book, *The Boxcar Children*, quickly proved she had succeeded.

Miss Warner drew on her own experiences to write the mystery. As a child she spent hours watching trains go by on the tracks opposite her family home. She often dreamed about what it would be like to set up housekeeping in a caboose or freight car — the situation the Alden children find themselves in.

When Miss Warner received requests for more adventures involving Henry, Jessie, Violet, and Benny Alden, she began additional stories. In each, she chose a special setting and introduced unusual or eccentric characters who liked the unpredictable.

While the mystery element is central to each of Miss Warner's books, she never thought of them as strictly juvenile mysteries. She liked to stress the Aldens' independence and resourcefulness and their solid New England devotion to using up and making do. The Aldens go about most of their adventures with as little adult supervision as possible — something else that delights young readers.

Miss Warner lived in Putnam, Connecticut, until her death in 1979. During her lifetime, she received hundreds of letters from girls and boys telling her how much they liked her books.